Adventures in Extreme Reading

THE CALM BEFORE THE STORM

#2

A NIGHT IN SLEEPY HOLLOW

magic
wagon

BY Jan Fields

visit us at www.abdopublishing.com

Published by Magic Wagon, a division of the ABDO Group,
PO Box 398166, Minneapolis, MN 55439. Copyright © 2013 by
Abdo Consulting Group, Inc. International copyrights reserved in all
countries. All rights reserved. No part of this book may be reproduced
in any form without written permission from the publisher.

Calico Chapter Books™ is a trademark and logo of Magic Wagon.

Printed in the United States of America, North Mankato, Minnesota.
102012
012013
 This book contains at least 10% recycled materials.

Written by Jan Fields
Cover illustration by Scott Altmann
Edited by Stephanie Hedlund and Grace Hansen
Cover and interior design by Neil Klinepier

Library of Congress Cataloging-in-Publication Data
Fields, Jan.
  The calm before the storm : a night in Sleepy Hollow / by Jan Fields ;
[illustrator, Scott Altmann].
    p. cm. -- (Adventures in extreme reading ; bk. 2)
  Summary: Carter Lewis is having trouble making it through The
legend of Sleepy Hollow, so his cousin, Isabelle, suggests that he use his
uncle's virtual reality machine to enter into the book as a character--
and meet the Headless Horseman up-close and personal.
  ISBN 978-1-61641-920-2
1. Irving, Washington, 1783-1859. Legend of Sleepy Hollow--Juvenile
fiction. 2. Virtual reality--Juvenile fiction. 3. Books and reading--
Juvenile fiction. 4. Inventions--Juvenile fiction. 5. Cousins--Juvenile
fiction. 6. Ghost stories. [1. Irving, Washington, 1783-1859. Legend
of Sleepy Hollow--Fiction. 2. Virtual reality--Fiction. 3. Books and
reading--Fiction. 4. Inventions--Fiction. 5. Cousins--Fiction. 6. Ghosts--
Fiction.] I. Altmann, Scott, ill. II. Title.
  PZ7.F479177Cal 2013
  813.6--dc23   2012028634

Table of Contents

HOMEWORK HORRORS

Carter Lewis yawned so wide his jaw cracked. He absolutely, positively had to get this book read before Monday. When his teacher assigned it, she had "pop quiz" written all over her face. Carter didn't dare crash and burn during another pop quiz.

He yawned again and wondered how anyone could think it was interesting to ramble on and on about how a town got its name. Who cares if Tarry Town used to be called Greensburgh? Besides, why talk about these other towns if the story takes place in Sleepy Hollow?

Carter knew there was supposed to be some kind of a chase scene. Ms. Mendelsong had peered over her glasses as she told the class, "Washington Irving's use of a supernatural

4

chase makes 'The Legend of Sleepy Hollow' similar to folktales of the time." She'd said a bunch of other stuff too, but that was all Carter remembered.

Carter wasn't sure he'd ever get to the chase, since he couldn't get past the first page with its description of the quietest place in the whole world. Who wanted to read about the quietest place in the whole world? He was hoping for a good zombie attack or maybe vampires swooping down on someone. Even a werewolf would be okay as long as it actually chased someone down and ate him. He groaned and tossed the book onto his desk. At least it was Friday. He still had two days to slog through the story before class on Monday.

Carter jumped when the pocket of his cargo shorts rattled against his leg. He'd put his new cell phone on vibrate because he was grounded. Technically, he wasn't supposed to use the phone, but how could a guy live like that?

"Hey," he said quietly.

"It's Isabelle. You need to come to Uncle Dan's house tomorrow."

"Oh, I'm fine," Carter said. "Just enjoying being grounded. And how are you, Izzy?"

His cousin groaned. "Just come to Uncle Dan's tomorrow."

"Why? Is he back?" Carter asked eagerly.

"No, he's still tracking down the guy who hacked his virtual reality program," Isabelle replied. "Apparently, Storm is pretty hard to find, even with Uncle Dan's connections. But that doesn't matter. I finished clearing out all the bad code. The program's clean, and I found something cool. I need you to come over so we can test it."

Carter frowned. Isabelle's definition of cool tended to be pretty different from a normal person's. Not that it mattered really. He sighed. "Can't. Grounded. Ms. Mendelsong sent home a note about my 'lack of preparation' in her class. And Mom is patrolling downstairs while Dad works outside. I can't manage a prison break this time."

"This kind of thing wouldn't happen if you did your reading," Isabelle said in her most annoying know-it-all voice.

"No one normal could read this stuff," Carter complained. "Anyway, I have to finish 'The Legend of Sleepy Hollow' before Monday. My Spidey sense is telling me she's going to hit us with a pop quiz or an instant essay on Monday. If I flunk another Mendelsong surprise, I'm going to be grounded until Christmas."

"How far have you gotten?"

Carter thought about lying, but then he decided he didn't care what Izzy thought. "I'm almost through the first page."

"Oh, come on," his cousin said. "That's a cool story. It's got a ghost and one of the first literary nerds. It's fun."

"The first page isn't," Carter answered.

"Hey, I have a great idea," Isabelle said. "Tell your folks you're meeting me so we can work on your English homework. They'll like that."

"You're suggesting I lie?" Carter said. "I'm shocked."

"Sure you are," she said. "But this isn't a lie. I can help you with your homework. 'The Legend of Sleepy Hollow' is one of the books in Uncle Dan's program. Once you've lived the book, you'll breeze through reading it."

A smile spread across Carter's face. He could imagine the big A inked across a pop quiz and putting an end to his grounding. Then the smile slipped.

"Are you sure you got all the mutant killer rabbits and crazy weather references out of the books?" he asked. "Wonderland was a little too intense for me last time we played with Uncle Dan's invention."

"You worry too much," Isabelle said. When Carter didn't answer, she finally added. "Yes, I ran a diagnostic three times. The books are clean. Now do you want a good grade or not?"

Carter sighed. Killer rabbits or not, he wanted a good grade. "I'll see you in the morning."

The next morning, Carter rode his bike to his uncle's house. He looked for the spare key, but Izzy hadn't put it back. Grumbling, he hiked his backpack higher on his shoulder and pressed his uncle's doorbell. He held his finger against the button until his cousin opened the door.

"That's obnoxious," she shouted over the door chimes ringing behind her. She shoved his hand off the button.

"So is not putting the key back."

Isabelle shrugged and backed up so Carter could pass. "I guess your parents thought studying together was a good idea."

"Yeah, yeah, they love you," he said. "Though that is the last time I voluntarily bring up your name and homework in the same conversation."

"You know, it would take less energy to just do your homework than it does to avoid it."

Carter glared at Izzy. "Thanks for the advice, Mom. Now, didn't you mention discovering something cool?" He seriously doubted anything Izzy found was really interesting, but it had to be better than more nagging.

Izzy's face lit up. "Right, come on!" She barreled down the stairs and called out the password to open their uncle's lab door.

Carter followed her through the door and looked around. His uncle's usual casual mayhem was gone. Clearly Isabelle had done more than work on their uncle's program. The room was almost blindingly clean. All of the monitors, tables, and keyboards were lined up with military precision on their tables.

"What did you do to this place?" Carter asked. "Uncle Dan is going to throw a fit."

Isabelle waved her hand as she slipped into Uncle Dan's computer chair. "I couldn't work in so much chaos. He'll love it."

Carter couldn't imagine his paranoid uncle loving quite so much change in his sacred computer room. But he knew better than to try to argue with Izzy.

"So what is the cool thing?" he asked instead.

"Look!" She pointed at the code on the

screen.

"Let's assume I don't want to read all that and just tell me."

Isabelle snorted. "It shows two different modes for experiencing the book program. We can enter the books as observers like you did with *The Three Musketeers* and *Alice in Wonderland* last time. But you can also choose to enter as a character that all the other characters will recognize."

"You did that last time," Carter said. "You played Alice."

She shook her head. "I overwrote Alice. That's different and it freaked the program out. This is different. We won't be an existing character. We'll be 'written in' as new characters."

Carter frowned. He didn't see the big deal.

"It'll be fun. Trust me."

"As long as it helps me pass the test on Monday," he said.

"It will," Isabelle assured him. "Just remember

the characters we'll be playing don't really exist in the book. But everything else should be perfectly normal. This is going to be a blast."

"We're both going in at once?" Carter said. "Is that safe?"

"Yes, yes." Isabelle began typing in a flurry. "'The Legend of Sleepy Hollow' is actually a short story. Once the story runs to the end, it'll just dump us out. Easy peasy."

Carter shuddered. He remembered just how badly his "easy peasy" jaunt into Wonderland had gone last time.

"Hey, does anyone in this book cut off people's heads?" he asked.

Izzy giggled at Carter's question but didn't answer.

Suddenly, Carter wondered if he should have just stayed home and read the book.

MEETING ICHABOD CRANE

Izzy's fingers flew over the keyboard for another minute before she hopped up and headed for what used to be a big basement storage room. Now it housed the two virtual reality suits their uncle had invented.

The room looked just the same as it had the last time Carter was in there, except a little cleaner. The bulky suits looked like they belonged in space, not hanging by dozens of cables from the ceiling like gigantic puppets.

"The program will begin automatically ten seconds after both suits are sealed," Izzy said as she opened the back of one suit. "We might not start off in the same place, but I'm sure I'll see you eventually."

"Are you sure that's a good idea?" Carter said. "Last time things went bad after we separated."

"You worry too much," Isabelle said again as she disappeared into the suit.

Carter sighed and climbed into his own suit. As the back sealed behind him, he felt the familiar burst of claustrophobia from the close darkness. He closed his eyes and started counting down in his head.

Ten, nine, eight, seven . . . He fought the urge to pant and reminded himself that he had plenty of air.

Six, five, four, three . . .

"Carter!" A voice called out. Carter snapped his eyes open and blinked against the bright light. "Carter Van Ripper!"

"Huh?" Carter turned to see a group of guys trotting toward him across a small clearing. They were all broad-shouldered and looked a little older, but only one was taller than Carter. The tall guy had short, curly black hair and a grin that stretched across his face.

"Carter Van Ripper," he repeated, "just the man I wanted to see."

Carter wasn't sure what to say, so he stood watching as they quickly closed the distance. The leader pounded Carter on the back in a good-natured way that seemed sure to leave bruises.

"How can I help you?" Carter asked hesitantly.

"Well, we have need of a bit of spying on that scarecrow of a schoolmaster," the tallest boy said.

"And seeing as you're clearly headed to the schoolhouse," one of his companions said, pointing at a book Carter just realized he held in his hands. "You seem prime for the job."

"I'm going to school?" Carter yelped, dropping the book. "No, I'm not."

"Ah, a man after my own heart," the tallest said agreeably as one of the others picked up the book and shoved it back in Carter's hands. "But I was hoping you would make the sacrifice today. You'd make a sure friend of Brom Bones if you would." The young man thumped himself on the chest. The gesture made it clear he was the Brom Bones in question.

"How is my going to school going to help you?" Carter asked.

"As I mentioned," Brom said, "I have need of a spy to watch Schoolmaster Crane. Since he is staying with your family and none of us would be welcome in his classroom . . ." Brom's two companions hooted at that idea. "We hoped you'd help a bit."

"What kind of spying do you want me to do?" Carter asked.

"I've heard tell that Schoolmaster Crane is the sort to believe in wild tales," Brom said. "But I was hoping you could find out what kind of devil's creature scares the man most."

"Why?"

"Why?" Brom opened his eyes wide in surprise. "Because it's time that prancing dandy was showed up for the coward he is. Then maybe some folks will come to their senses about Mr. Ichabod Crane. But enough talk. We don't want you to be late for your lessons. I know Schoolmaster Crane is handy with his cane."

Carter wasn't sure what a cane had to do with school, but Brom gave him a friendly shove that sent him staggering. He decided to get going before his new buddy knocked him down.

The three older boys hooted encouragement as Carter hurried along, following a brook that wove along through the small valley. The air was cool and had the dusty smell of fall. Carter heard chirps and hoots from the nearby trees. A flock of wild ducks flew over, quacking at one another as they held their sharp formation.

Soon he came to a dirt road where the brook took a slow turn. He wasn't sure which way to take after that. With a sigh, he picked the one that continued in the same direction as the brook, since that direction kept the sun out of his eyes.

Eventually he spotted a rough log cabin that

stood at the foot of a woody hill. The building had a scattering of small windows. Only a few of the windows had glass, the rest were patched with pages from old books. At one end of the schoolhouse, a gold-leafed birch tree grew, giving a little shade from the sun.

"I can't believe I have to go to school on a Saturday," Carter grumbled as he hauled open the heavy wooden door. He stepped into the long, narrow room. With one glance, Carter could tell he was going to be the tallest kid in this dinky class. The two boys in the front row were so little, their legs dangled from the shared bench where they sat. Their feet didn't touch the ground.

The narrow building was filled with rows of benches and rough desks. Each desk had it's own inkwell. The boys looked up from their writing or reading and stared at Carter.

"So, Master Van Ripper has decided to join us after all!"

Carter turned toward the voice and gawked.

A man slightly taller than Carter stood between a high stool and a battered desk. The desktop was nearly covered with half-munched apples, popguns, and notched sticks with propellers. Just beyond the desk, near the front corner of the room, a long, narrow, rough-hewed door hung. It was marked with a gouged x.

The glaring man cleared his throat, jerking Carter's attention back toward him. He seemed impossibly thin in his baggy clothes with too short sleeves. The combination of short pants and tall stockings made his scrawny legs look like twigs.

The man's small head perched on a long neck. The huge ears sticking out from each side of the flat-topped head would have been all you noticed if it had not been for the nose. The schoolmaster's nose pointed at Carter like the beak of a bad-tempered stork.

Carter had to fight down a bark of laughter just looking at the guy. He realized this must be the Ichabod Crane that he was supposed to spy on.

"Sorry," Carter said. "Didn't mean to be late."

Schoolmaster Crane stared at Carter in shock. His big knuckled hand reached out and snatched a long stick from the wall where it rested on three nails.

"That is hardly a proper way to address your schoolmaster," Crane said, swishing the green stick through the air.

Carter realized the funny-looking man intended to hit him with the stick. "Now just hold on!" he yelped.

"Schoolmaster Crane?" a familiar voice sounded from the middle of the room. Both Crane and Carter turned to look at Izzy, who stood at attention beside one of the benches. She wore boys' clothes similar to those worn by Crane. "I believe someone is coming, sir. It appears to be one of Father's servants, sir."

"Oh!" Crane said as he quickly reseated the lashing stick on its three-nail perch. "Well, do sit down, Master Van Ripper."

Izzy waved and Carter hurried down the aisle to join her on the bench. She flipped open a book and he opened the one he'd been carrying. A knock sounded at the door and Crane rushed to pull the door open.

The man at the door wore a jacket and pants made from cheap linen covered with fuzzy spots. A battered hat with a round top sat on his short, black curls.

"Schoolmaster Crane," the man announced loudly as he swept the hat from his head with a nervous hand, "you are formally invited to attend an evening of merry-making and quilting frolic at the home of Mynheer Van Tassel."

Before Ichabod Crane could say a word, the man turned sharply and rushed out. He climbed on the bare back of a ragged wild colt that danced and dashed as if hoping to unseat the rider. But the servant only leaned into the ride and clutched the rope he used for a halter. The horse splashed through the brook and up the hill.

"Well," Crane said in a cheery tone as he lifted the lashing stick off the nails again, "let me check over your copybooks and I believe we'll be done for the day. You have all worked so hard." Isabelle quickly swapped copybooks with Carter, then bent over and began filling the pages with words at blinding speed.

As the teacher bent over each desk, he reminded Carter of a praying mantis waiting for a chance to nip off someone's head. He stalked up the aisle and loomed over one of the boys whose feet dangled above the floor.

"You should have finished this by now," he snapped. "Clearly you need more encouragement. Stand!"

All around the room, boys dropped their eyes to their books as if they were glued there. Only Carter stared at Ichabod Crane. He couldn't believe the schoolmaster intended to hit the little kid with his stick. He started to edge out of his seat when Izzy caught his arm.

"The kids aren't real," she whispered. "This

is just a computer simulation."

"I don't care," he whispered back through gritted teeth, tugging his arm away from Isabelle.

"Schoolmaster Crane," Izzy said suddenly.

Ichabod Crane's head turned on his long spindle neck.

"My sister, Katrina, was just telling me how important it is to her that the man she marries be kind to children," Isabelle said. "And gentle. I didn't tell her differently, but my sister is so trusting. I know she would believe the word of her little brother."

Crane's eyes narrowed. "Are you threatening me?"

"No, sir," Izzy said. "Only sharing how much my dear sister values kindness and honesty. I try always to be honest. Do you try always to be kind, sir?"

The lanky teacher was nearly shaking with rage at Isabelle. But he shoved the small boy back into his seat and stalked toward their table. He bent over their desk and snatched up

Carter's book, his bulgy eyes sweeping over the neat writing.

"Well," he said, "you are a wonder, Master Van Ripple. This is nicely done."

Then he turned his hawk-nose toward Izzy. "And what do you have, Master Van Tassel?"

"It might be a bit wobbly," Isabelle said. "My dear sister often scolds me for my wobbly writing."

Ichabod Crane barely glanced at the copybook. "Yes, your dear sister. I look forward to seeing her tonight at the festivities."

"She has told me how much she looks forward to seeing you, as well," Isabelle said.

Crane's rage seemed to melt away at that. He stood and moved dreamily to the next student.

"Why are you dressed like a boy?" Carter whispered.

Izzy cut an alarmed glance toward Crane, but it was clear you couldn't have gotten the distracted schoolmaster's attention with a thrown rock.

"Girls never do anything in these old books," she whispered. "So I'm Isaiah Van Tassel."

Carter looked at her and shook his head. "You don't look like a boy. You're just dressed like a boy."

"I look like a boy to the book characters." She glanced at Ichabod Crane again. "Now, hush, we'll be out of here soon."

We better be, Carter thought. He still intended to yell at her for making them go to school, especially when the teacher was clearly stick happy. This story better get more exciting fast!

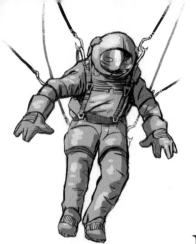

PRANKS IN THE HOLLOW

Isabelle turned out to be right. Crane barely glanced at the rest of the class's work. He waved his stick around once or twice, but he didn't actually hit anyone with it.

When he looked up from the last student, he announced, "You've done fine work today. I believe you deserve an early dismissal. Good afternoon to you all!" Then Crane strode back to the front of the room, picked up a small bell from his desk, and rang it.

Isabelle put her books away neatly, but everyone else flung them aside. The two boys in the row ahead jumped up so fast their bench fell over. It was left there as the boys stampeded the door, yelping and laughing.

That was the first time Carter noticed that Isabelle was the only girl in the class.

"Do girls go to a different school?" he asked her as he stood up.

"Most girls don't go to school at all," she said with a sniff.

"Luck-ee!" Carter sang out, and Izzy just looked at him with disgust.

"In this part of history, women were considered the property of their fathers until they were unloaded on a husband," she said. "They didn't need school because they were barely considered people!"

Carter raised his hands in surrender. "Okay, okay. Don't bite my head off."

"Master Van Tassel, Master Van Ripper," Ichabod Crane called. He peered in a piece of broken mirror that hung on the wall near his desk and fussed over his thin hair. "I appreciate your clear love of the classroom, but you need to leave so I can secure the building. The last time I left a window loose, some ruffians slipped in and turned the place topsy-turvy."

He made shooing gestures at Carter and Izzy that made him look like a cranky chicken. Carter had to fight back a laugh as he hurried out the door.

"No more school!" he huffed as they headed up the narrow road.

"Don't worry," she said. "We won't be back."

"So, where do we go now?"

"Well, you'll go to your house, and I'll go to mine."

Carter frowned. "I have no idea where my house is."

"Where did you start out when you popped into the program?" she asked.

Carter pointed. "I was just in a field."

"If you head back that way," she said, "you should end up at your house. The program will make sure of it. Especially if you say something that shows where you're headed. It adapts."

"How do you know that?"

"I just spent a week wading through the guts

of the base program," she said with a shrug. "I noticed a few things."

"What am I supposed to do when I get home?"

"Ichabod Crane is staying at your house. You could follow him when he heads for the party. That's where the real action happens," Isabelle answered. "I'll see you at the party, since it's going to be at my house."

"I'm not letting that guy hit me," he said.

"Don't worry," she answered. "He's Mister Super Nice in front of parents. He'll treat you like you're his best friend."

Carter sniffed. "So he's a big fake."

"Right," Izzy said. "But he's also dependent on the farmers around here for room and board. He can't afford to make waves. And he's hoping to marry Katrina Van Tassel so he'll have money and freedom. Then he'll quit teaching and travel. At least, that's what he dreams of."

"How do you know that?"

She gave him the look. "I read the story."

"Well," Carter said, "Brom Bones seems to

think this guy is a big weenie."

"You know about Brom Bones?" Isabelle's eyes grew round.

"I met him on the way to school," Carter said. "He wants me to spy on Crane."

"Oh, that is so cool!" Isabelle said. "Maybe he'd like me to help, too."

"Aren't you his girlfriend's brother?" Carter asked. "Would Brom want her to know what he's doing?"

Izzy slumped. "Probably not. Well, that stinks. Okay, I'm going back 'home,' but you have to tell me everything later, okay?"

Carter shrugged. "Sure." He pointed to the sharp bend in the creek. "This is where I turn if I'm supposed to walk the way I did this morning."

She nodded and turned to go. Carter watched her head up the road from the schoolhouse. He followed the brook and headed up the hill. When he was pretty sure he was near the spot where he started in the program, he said, "Well, here I am going home!" He felt a little goofy talking to the air, but he wanted to make sure the program didn't think he wanted to wander around in the countryside all day.

As he topped a small hill, he saw Brom Bones. Brom was on the back of a horse, racing up and down a strip of grassy field. When Brom caught sight of Carter, he raced the horse toward him. For a moment, Carter considered running as the huge black horse thundered toward him, but Brom pulled hard on the reins and the horse came to a snorting halt.

Brom held out a hand. "Afternoon, friend. Can I give you a lift?"

Carter had never ridden a horse, but he grabbed Brom's hand and let the older boy haul him up onto the saddle behind him.

"So how is our dandy scarecrow today?" Brom called over his shoulder. "Did you make it to school?"

"I did," he said. "Then Schoolmaster Crane received an invitation to the Van Tassel's tonight.

He closed the school early."

"Of course he would," Brom grumbled, but then his voice brightened. "So do you want to give a friend a hand with a bit of a prank?"

Carter grinned. He loved pranks. "What do you need me to do?"

"I could use a good mind," Brom said. "Imagine a fellow wanted to cover up the dashing white socks on old Daredevil here. How would you do that?" Brom patted the horse's neck fondly.

Carter thought about it. "You could use paint or ink."

"True," Brom said. "But it's hard to come by and wouldn't wash off quickly. Imagine a person needed to bring the socks back without too much effort."

"Will they have to look black in good light or close-up?" Carter asked.

"No. What I have in mind would happen at night."

"How about mud?"

Brom burst out with a roar of laughter. "Why didn't I think of that?" he asked. "I knew you'd be a good partner in this, my friend. Now, what's say we go spy on Mr. Ichabod Crane? I'm ready for another good laugh." Brom turned his horse sharply and galloped across the rocky meadow at a rump-busting speed.

Brom slowed down just as Carter began wondering whether he was ever going to be able to sit down again after their little ride. Daredevil slipped into a shadowy patch of trees. They wove between the thin tree trunks with surprisingly little sound.

Finally Brom pointed. "There's the dandy."

Carter blinked at the bright sunlight beyond the woods. He saw the lanky schoolteacher marching along, singing some gloomy song.

"Don't he look ready to take the world by storm?" Brom grumbled.

"At least you've got a horse," Carter said. "He has to walk everywhere."

Brom looked at him sharply. "Good point.

He needs a horse." Brom narrowed his eyes as he thought about it. "I have an idea. You hop off and walk a bit with our dandy friend. Suggest he borrow your father's horse to impress Katrina. Tell him how much she's always admired Gunpowder."

"I don't want to hang out with that guy," Carter protested. "He smacks little kids with a stick."

"Surely you're not afraid of him?"

"Hardly."

"Then go on with you," Brom said, helping Carter from the horse. "Be sure Ichabod Crane ends up on Gunpowder tonight. I'm counting on you."

With that, Brom Bones turned Daredevil sharply and headed quickly through the trees. Carter watched them go, then he sighed.

"I knew I hated this book," he muttered as he tromped out of the woods toward the schoolmaster.

PREPARING THE DANDY

"**W**ell, Master Van Ripper, I am surprised you are not yet at home," Ichabod Crane said when Carter caught up to him.

"I, uh, got caught up with a friend," Carter said. He was shorter than Crane, and had some trouble matching the schoolmaster's long-legged stride. "But I'm heading home now."

"Good, good," Crane said cheerfully. "Families are the Nurseries of all Societies; and the First combinations of Mankind."

"Huh?"

"Words of wisdom from the great Cotton Mather," Crane said. "You would do well to read and learn from such wisdom. I can loan you a book if you like."

"Oh, yeah, maybe sometime," Carter said, not

sure how to respond. He decided against asking what kind of weird people would name their kid *Cotton*. For a few minutes, he concentrated on walking without panting. He tried to think of some way to turn the conversation toward the party.

"You look nice," Carter finally mumbled. "Your hair is all slick and, um, shiny. I'm sure Katrina will like that."

"Thank you." The schoolmaster looked at Carter suspiciously.

Carter took a deep breath. "Have you thought of how you'll get to the party?"

Again, the schoolmaster looked at him through narrowed eyes. "I expect I shall use the same mode of transportation that I presently employ."

"Huh?"

"I shall walk. And you should respond to conversation with words, not the breathy sounds of a wheezing horse."

"Right," Carter said, beginning to wonder

exactly why he was having this conversation in the first place. "Speaking of horses, you know Brom Bones will be riding Daredevil. Girls like horses."

Ichabod Crane frowned. "I have no horse."

"No," Carter admitted. "But my . . . um . . . my father has a horse named Gunpowder. He's even better than Daredevil. You could probably borrow him."

The schoolmaster's face lit up. "That does sound fine. You have done me a good deed, Master Van Ripper. And as Cotton Mather says, 'Our opportunities to do good are our talents.'"

Crane was clearly so happy over the idea of riding Gunpowder that he picked up his pace until Carter practically had to run to keep up. Between the panting and the wheezing, Carter didn't try any more conversation. That seemed fine with the schoolteacher, who galloped along with a goofy smile on his face.

They climbed one more small hill, and Carter spotted a house with a steeply leaning barn.

He assumed this was "home" and slowed down sharply. Ichabod hurried toward the house without a single glance back at Carter.

Carter wasn't at all sure he wanted to meet his "father" in this book. Didn't kids have to work every day after school back in the old days? He wasn't eager to spend a few hours shoveling horse poop or weeding corn or whatever a kid had to do in the fall here.

He crept closer to the house, trying to keep out of sight of the windows. He found a good hiding place behind a barrel near the barn and squatted down to wait. His shady hiding spot was cool, though the fragrant scent of horse wafted from the barn behind him. It made Carter even more determined to avoid poop shoveling.

Eventually, the long shadow of the barn had stretched until it nearly touched the house. Carter knew it must be late afternoon. It didn't feel like he'd been sitting all that long, so Carter suspected the program compressed time when nothing much happened.

He was startled by the sound of voices and peeked around the barrel. He spotted Ichabod Crane striding toward the barn beside a broad man with a scowling red face.

"Where is that boy of mine?" the man demanded.

"I do not know, sir," Crane said. "We walked a ways together after school let out, but I lost sight of him. I assumed he was off to do chores."

The man snorted but said no more on the subject. The two walked into the barn.

"Wow," Carter muttered. "Even my fake dad is on my case."

Carter scooted along the side of the barn so he could peer inside. It was difficult to make out more than shapes in the darkness. It was easy enough to make out the silhouette of the lanky schoolteacher and the wider farmer. They stood before a stall door. Carter could hear angry snorting and stomping coming from inside.

In a few minutes, Carter could see both men dragging a horse in his direction, so he bolted back behind the barrel. Soon the men burst into the light with the oddest horse Carter had ever seen. It was stomping and tossing its head.

The horse was scrawny with a thin, curved neck. Its mane and tail were the color of dead leaves, and it had quite a few bits of leaf and stick caught up in its knotted tail. As the horse thrashed its head, Carter saw one eye looked milky white and blind. The other rolled in its socket with crazy temper. It looked like the kind of horse that would bite and kick with equal meanness.

"He's seen a bit of work in his day," Van Ripper said proudly. "But he's still my favorite. This is a horse with spirit!"

Crane eyed the horse nervously. "Spirit is good, I suppose. I want to make a fine entrance."

"You'll be a proud figure on this horse, lad," the farmer said. He smacked the horse on the shoulder hard enough to make it lash out at him, snapping yellow teeth. "Take a firm hand though, lad. Gunpowder can be the devil indeed."

"I'll heed your words," the schoolteacher said as he climbed awkwardly into the saddle. He turned the horse toward a dusty trail leading away from the farm. Soon, he was bouncing along in the saddle.

Van Ripper watched a moment, then shook his head and turned toward the house. Carter waited until the man was inside, then turned to follow Ichabod Crane.

"I don't know how I'm supposed to keep up with a horse," he muttered. Then he wondered if it would help to tell the program where he wanted to go. Feeling silly again, he announced, "I'm headed to the party." Nothing magical happened so he sighed and walked quickly along the same dusty trail the schoolteacher had taken.

Carter realized he seemed to be walking really fast, or at least covering a lot of ground. He figured it was more book magic. That was fine with him. He didn't like the idea of spending an hour hiking to the party.

He passed through a small apple orchard. The sweet smell of ripe apples hung in the air and every tree was full of fruit. He passed baskets and barrels piled with apples.

After the apple orchard, he passed swiftly by browning corn fields and then a pumpkin patch. He passed fields with crops he didn't recognize. The shadows of late afternoon deepened still more as he walked. He picked up his pace to a trot, hoping to get to the party before dark.

Then he spotted the Van Tassel farm. A huge tree spread broad branches over the house itself. Carter saw a barn nearby that was clearly big enough to hold every building at the Van Ripper farm and the schoolhouse along with them. Though the barn was the larger building by far, it was clear the party was in the house. Carter could see people gathering at the door to enter, so he hurried along to join them.

The house was big with exposed ceiling beams where tools Carter couldn't identify hung up out of the way. Along the sides of the great room were benches where a number of people already sat and chattered. He spotted a spinning wheel in one corner and a butter churn in another. The doors to other rooms hung open and people passed from room to room, laughing and talking.

Nearly all of the men wore coats, knee-length pants, and tall blue stockings. The older women had their hair tucked up in simple caps and wore long dresses with brightly colored pockets hanging on a belt like an apron. Straw hats perched on the heads of the younger women and the young men had slicked their hair back into short, shiny ponytails.

Carter was looking around and feeling a bit overwhelmed when a friendly smack on the back sent him reeling toward the fireplace. "Friend Carter," Brom bellowed in a fierce stage whisper, "I see your task went well. I noticed your father's horse when I tied up Daredevil."

"It didn't take much convincing," Carter said.

"Still, good man," Brom said, throwing an arm around Carter's neck, half-choking him. "Come along and let's find something good to eat."

He dragged Carter across the room to a table heaped with platters of cakes. Carter recognized several kinds of crullers and his stomach growled. He also caught the scent of roast chicken, bringing on another fierce growl.

"You should eat before your stomach decides you are completely starved," Brom said. He grabbed a plate and began piling it high.

Carter doubted even Uncle Dan's brilliant virtual reality could make him feel full from virtual food. He looked around, hoping to spot Izzy so he could ask her what they should expect next.

He finally saw her through an open door. She was standing next to a round, cheerful man. He hustled her along with an arm around her shoulders while he shouted greetings at everyone he passed. Carter assumed that must be Isabelle's father in the story.

"Sure, she gets the happy dad," he muttered.

He started across the room toward her when a burst of fiddle music distracted him. A dark-haired girl in a straw hat decorated with blue ribbons suddenly slipped an arm through Carter's.

"Master Van Ripper," she said, "come and dance with me."

While he stammered and stumbled, she hauled him into a room crowded with young people. That's when he finally spotted Ichabod Crane. The lanky schoolteacher looked like every dancing movie nerd Carter had ever seen. Not a part of him was still as he danced. He looked like a loosely strung puppet being shaken hard so that arms and legs swung everywhere.

Carter looked to see who would be willing to dance with someone making a scene like that.

He saw a smiling girl with a round face and pink cheeks. He also spotted Brom Bones scowling at Crane and the girl, so he guessed she must be Katrina.

Then Carter's partner pulled him into the line and he forgot all about noticing anyone else. He stumbled and bumped folks around him during the complicated moves of the dance. At one point, he spun in a staggering circle and saw Izzy standing in the doorway, doubled over laughing.

Then Carter's dance partner jerked him back around and all he could do was plot revenge against his cousin for this whole idea.

GHOST STORIES

After being totally humiliated while dancing, Carter sighed with relief as the fiddler finally took a break. He spotted Ichabod heading for Katrina's father and started after them, but his giggling dance partner grabbed his arm and dragged him toward the food table.

"Farm girls are a lot stronger than I thought," he muttered.

Izzy headed them off. "Excuse me," she said. "I need to borrow your beau to ask his advice about a runny sore my mare has. The wound smells like a ten-day-old corpse."

The farm girl wrinkled her nose and let go of Carter's arm. "Pray, save the rest of your description for private, Isaiah."

"Sorry to offend," Isabelle said, though she

didn't look the least bit sorry.

"Thanks for the rescue," Carter said as they slipped through the crowd. "If I had to smell roast chicken again, I think I would have starved to death."

"Yeah," Isabelle agreed. "It must be past lunchtime in real time. I'm going to tell Uncle Dan he needs to build some kind of feeding system in these suits." She pulled Carter into a small room lined with crocks and barrels. "Okay, now tell me everything. What kind of prank did Brom want you to do?"

Carter shrugged. "Nothing yet. He asked me how to cover up white spots on a horse. And he told me to be sure Ichabod Crane rode Gunpowder tonight. That Gunpowder is one sorry looking horse."

"But he didn't ask you to come along?" she said, clearly disappointed.

"Not so far," Carter said. "But did you see his face when that nutty teacher was flopping all over the dance floor? I thought he was going to jump up and rip Crane's throat out." Then Carter's eyes grew wide. "Is that it? Is Brom some kind of werewolf in this story? That would be so cool."

"No," she said. "So tell me everything you've done so far without me."

Carter figured he owed his cousin that much since she had saved him from the clutches of the world's strongest giggling farm girl. He told her about riding with Brom Bones.

"You got to ride Daredevil?" Izzy yelped. "That is so cool."

"I guess," Carter agreed. Then he launched into a description of lurking around the farm while Ichabod Crane got the horse. "By the way, how come I get the grumpy, frog-faced dad, and you get the smiling, friendly dad?"

She shrugged. "Hey, eventually they're going to be telling ghost stories over where the men are smoking. We should go hear them."

"Now that sounds like a party," Carter said.

They gave the food table plenty of room as

they passed by. Carter kept a sharp eye out for his would-be girlfriend, but they made it over to the smoky corner of the great room without anyone grabbing him. Ichabod Crane sat among the farmers, looking mildly bored as he listened to their stories.

" . . . And as the musket ball came at him, he brought his small sword up to block that smoking ball of death," said an older man. He spoke with a pipe clenched in his teeth, giving his words an odd lisp. "He felt it whiz round the blade and glance off the hilt. I know it's true. I've seen the sword in question and the hilt is bent from the blow."

"As much as I enjoy these wild war tales," Ichabod Crane finally interrupted, "I've heard that you have far more frightening happenings in these hills and homes than old soldier stories. Have I not heard of witches and ghosts stalking the night?"

"Aye, we have such," agreed another. "There's something dark in the very air that blows from

Sleepy Hollow. I myself have heard the shrieking of the woman in white. And every time she howls, I know to bring my cattle in close, for a storm will blow to kill the toughest bull."

"You've only heard her?" shouted the farmer with the pipe in his teeth. "I've seen her at the dark glen at Raven Rock. As thin as smoke with black pits for eyes. She visits my dreams, reaching for me with those bone-white fingers."

"That's no ghost in your dreams," Brom Bones called as he joined the group, grinning. "That's your wife. You need to feed that woman!"

A chorus of laughs and shouts followed his remark. Even the farmer's scowl finally broke and he chuckled at the younger man.

Ichabod Crane sniffed. "If you were an educated man who had read the writings of the brilliant Cotton Mather, you would know better than to jest! Clearly this white woman is a witch or the ghost of a witch."

"Maybe she's your mother," Brom said with another braying laugh. "She's skinny enough!"

This brought another roar of laughter from the gathered men, and the schoolmaster sat back with his arms crossed and a scowl on his face.

"Don't you believe in ghosts at all, lad?" Van Tassel asked from where he sat at the very center of the men.

"I do, sir," Brom said, looking sideways at Ichabod Crane and dropping his voice to a loud whisper. "For I've seen one. I've seen the Hessian who grazes his demon horse among the graves of the churchyard."

"The Headless Horseman," several of the men whispered hoarsely.

Carter jumped. He'd heard of the Headless Horseman. Was that this book? "Cool," he whispered as he crowded in on the end of one of the long benches. Finally, something interesting was happening at this party.

"You know the church of which I speak, of course," Brom said. "In day, it is a place of sunbeams and peace up on its knoll. Locust trees and lofty elms give gentle shade to the slumbering dead. Not far from the church lies the rocky brook splashing along its way. In day, it is a lovely spot."

"But not at night," a gravel-voiced farmer croaked. Then he shuddered.

"Nay," Brom said, dropping his voice to a hoarse whisper. All the men leaned forward slightly to better hear the story. Carter noticed that Ichabod Crane's eyes got wider and wider as Brom spoke. "At night the shadows seem to snatch at any who dare ride upon the rocky road nearby. And only the truly brave would cross the bridge that spans the brook, for the trees cast such shadow over the bridge that it looks like the very crossing point to the afterlife itself."

"'Tis a fearful dark place," agreed the farmer, his voice choked.

"I heard tell," said the farmer with the pipe in his teeth, "that there was a farmer named Brouwer who swore ghosts were nothing but hard drink and foolishness. He ran into the

Horseman. The foul creature pulled him up into the saddle of that demon horse and road like the hounds of the devil were on his tail. Then when the Horseman reached the bridge, his flesh fell away like rotten pumpkin. When the Horseman was nothing but bones, he threw old Brouwer into the brook."

"And old Brouwer's hair turned white as snow," the gravel-voiced farmer added. "And for the rest of his life, he shook like a man in the grip of fever."

The group of men nodded silently for a moment. Carter could tell they all knew the story of Brouwer well. Then Brom Bones burst into harsh laughter so loud that Ichabod Crane nearly tumbled from his spot on the bench in surprise.

"I've no fear of such a foolish jockey as the Horseman. What kind of ghost cannot even keep up with his own head?" Brom said. Among his audience, some of the men chortled along with Brom. Others looked all the more nervous for Brom's mocking.

"'Tis easy to mock what you have not seen," Crane said in his high, nasal voice.

"Are you deaf, man?" Brom demanded, leaning close to the schoolmaster's long nose. "I have seen the Horseman. What's more, I've raced him."

A collective gasp went up from the group. Carter looked around and caught Izzy's eye as she leaned against a nearby wall. It was clear that only Izzy and he suspected Brom was about to make up a seriously tall tale.

"Tell us," whispered the farmer, who now clenched his pipe in two hands instead of his teeth.

"I was coming home late one night from Sing Sing," he began.

Carter looked at Isabelle and mouthed, "Sing Sing?"

"Village," she mouthed back. "Nearby."

He nodded and turned back to the dark-haired storyteller. "I was riding Daredevil. As you might know, there is no faster horse in all of this fine world. The night was fearsome dark with no moon to brighten the sky. Even the stars had stopped their winking."

Brom paused and looked over his audience, smiling. Then he leaned forward again. "I heard the sounds of hooves behind me, and I was glad for the thought of company. The hoofbeats pounded so hard that I expected the rider to rush past me at any moment. Then he appeared—the Horseman!"

Ichabod Crane gave a small shriek that brought every eye toward him. He tried to cover his outburst with a cough. The farmers' grins made it plain they weren't fooled. Brom's smile looked less amused and more secretive to Carter. There was no doubt his new friend was telling this story especially for Ichabod Crane. Was he just trying to frighten the scrawny schoolmaster, or did he have more in mind?

BROM'S RACE

Soon the chuckles died down. All eyes turned back to Brom Bones for the rest of his story.

"As I said, the Horseman caught up to me at an otherworldly speed," he said. "But he didn't pass. Instead, he rode along at my side for a bit. He wore the winter wools of a Hessian soldier with a thick, dark cape flung over his shoulders. His horse was even blacker than the night, though when he snorted, the breath glowed with the very fires of Satan himself.

"I waited to see if the Horseman might speak to me. He did not, but then, he had no mouth to speak nor head to hold such a mouth."

Once again, Brom had everyone's attention. Carter had to admit, the combination of his low, harsh whisper and pauses for effect were pretty spooky.

"I knew if we were to share conversation, I would need to begin it," Brom said. "I nodded and said, 'You ride a fine horse, Sir Specter. I believe he is nearly as fine a horse as my own Daredevil.'

"Well, the Horseman didn't like that at all. His horse reared up and pawed the air as if to strike sparks against the night itself. I must admit, I felt a twinge of worry then."

Nods and shudders went through the audience.

"We rode on still farther in silence before I said, 'I know a way to show my Daredevil's speed. Let us race, Sir Specter.' The Horseman must have been willing for his horse reared again before striking the road running."

Now the farmers looked disapproving of the Horseman who clearly cheated at the race by jumping the gun. "He might have run fair and square," the gravel-voice farmer scolded.

"He might have, but he did not," Brom said. "Still, Daredevil must have taken it as an insult, for I have never seen my horse run as he ran that night. He overtook that evil nag the Horseman rode and we ran side by side for nearly a mile before Daredevil pulled out in front. There was no doubt we would win this race."

Then he stopped and looked around the group.

"So?" Crane squeaked. "Did you?"

"We would have," Brom said. "We surely would. We beat that goblin horse all through the hollow." Then he paused again and took a deep breath. "Then just as we reached the church bridge, that Hessian vanished in a flash of fire."

"A trick," the farmer with the pipe scoffed. "I would call you the winner."

"Nay," the gravel-voice farmer insisted. "The Hessian was toying with the lad. He could have used those demon powers to win at any point."

"That's the trick," the other insisted.

Carter leaned back and watched Ichabod Crane as the farmers squabbled about whether Brom really won the imaginary race. The schoolmaster looked pale. He had twisted his hands so tightly together that his long fingers looked like knots.

"Well, I'm up for a rematch if ever the Horseman wants one!" Brom said.

"You shouldn't mock," Crane said, his voice shaky. "Surely mockery can anger the spirits. Who knows when they might take revenge!"

Brom laughed. "Are you worried, schoolmaster? Do you imagine the Horseman will ride up behind you tonight as you canter home on Van Ripper's ragged beast? Perhaps the Horseman's stead will snort in your ear and turn your slicked-down hair white."

"That's not funny!" Crane nearly whimpered.

"From where I sit, 'tis very funny indeed," Brom said.

"That's because you are ignorant," Crane said. "If you had the wisdom of Cotton Mather in your thick head and had seen what I have seen on my walks about Sleepy Hollow, you'd not mock so easily."

"Ah, perhaps you could share this wisdom with us," Van Tassel said warmly. He was clearly trying to settle the tension between the two men.

"Thank you, sir," Ichabod Crane said as he pulled a ragged book from his deep jacket pocket. "I would be glad to read you a bit to show just how dangerous it can be to doubt the workings of the devil!"

Carter rolled his eyes. He'd already had enough of Cotton Mather from Crane. He looked at Izzy, but his cousin stared intently at the lanky schoolmaster. Naturally, she would be interested. He slumped against the wall and tuned in to Crane's reading for a minute.

"The children were tormented just in the same part of their bodies all at the same time together," the schoolmaster read. "And though they saw and heard not one another's complaints, though likewise their pains and sprains were swift like lightning . . ."

Carter groaned. There was no way he was listening to all that. He got up and clumped across the floor to find anything more interesting than that. He walked a little too close to the food table and the smell of roast meat sent his stomach rumbling again.

"When this is done, I'm having two lunches," he muttered. "Maybe three."

"You know, talking to yourself is a bad sign," Isabelle said from directly behind him.

Carter jumped and spun around. "Give a guy a heart attack why don't you?"

She shrugged and grinned. "That'll teach you to be alert. I think the party is going to break up soon. Then we'll have to follow Ichabod if we want to see the action."

"Is he really going to see the Headless Horseman?" Carter asked.

"Would I spoil the story for you?" she said.

"Well, if we don't get out of here soon,"

Carter said. "I'm eating my suit."

She shrugged. "We can wait outside if you want. I don't think anything else interesting is going to happen in here. And we should probably pick a horse."

"A horse?" Carter echoed.

"Yeah," she said. "We can't keep up with Ichabod by walking."

He hadn't thought about that. His backside still ached a little from the ride with Brom. Still, it would be worth it to see a ghost. He followed his cousin outside.

The night air was cooler, but it was better suited for the shirt and jacket Carter wore. It had grown stuffy in the house with so many people and the roaring fires. Carter followed Izzy to a jutting piece of rock that lay in the deep gloom under a huge chestnut tree.

"Maybe we could hop out of the suits, have lunch, then come back," Carter said.

Isabelle drummed the heels of her thick leather shoes on the side of the rock. "That would be a good idea, but I didn't build in any kind of exit mechanism. And if Uncle Dan made one, I don't know what it is."

"I thought you knew everything about these programs," Carter said.

"This is the most complex program I've ever seen," Isabelle said, her voice building into a rant. "It might be the most complex program ever written. I can't know everything, but I know a whole lot more than you. If you spent a half hour watching the code scroll in front of your eyes, your head would explode."

Carter held up a hand, "No double about it." He shifted a little, trying to find a spot where the hard boulder didn't mash any of the bruises he was sure he'd picked up earlier.

"So there could be something in there, even if you didn't see it," Carter said. "Uncle Dan wouldn't just leave people stuck forever. What if you're inside one of those horrible four-inch-thick books? You'd starve to death."

Izzy nodded, clearly calming down. "I agree.

Logically there must be an exit mechanism. I just don't know what it is."

Carter thought about how he got out of computer games. He yelled, "Control, alt, delete."

A young couple near the door of the house looked at them with puzzled frowns.

"Exit!" Carter commanded.

A farmer and his young family were coming out of the house as he shouted. The whole family turned to squint into the darkness at Carter and Izzy.

"You're going to get them thinking we're possessed," Isabelle whispered fiercely.

"I don't care, I need a sandwich," Carter whispered back. Then he sat up straight and yelled, "Escape!"

"From what?" a deep voice asked from the shadows beside them, making both Izzy and Carter jump. Brom Bones stepped close enough for Carter to make out his broad shoulders in the darkness. "You wouldn't be sending the schoolmaster a warning, now would you, lads?"

"No," Carter said. "It's Isaiah I wanted to escape from. He talks all the time."

Brom laughed. "Sounds like my little sister. She can chatter to set the magpies jealous."

"That was a great story you told," Carter said.

"Wasn't it though?" Brom agreed. "It set the schoolmaster's bones to knocking."

"Was it true?" Isabelle asked.

"Would I tell a lie in your father's house?" Brom asked. His white teeth flashed as he grinned at them. He turned to point toward the house. "Seems the party is breaking up."

Carter spotted the farm girl who had dragged him around the dance floor and sank back. She was walking out of the house, her face turned to look at someone inside. Then a young man, followed her and boldly put his arm around her waist. Isabelle leaned close to Carter and whispered, "It looks like your girlfriend didn't miss you."

"She wasn't my girlfriend," he growled back.

More couples and families lingered in the faint light from the house as farmers brought around the wagons to haul their families home.

As each group of guests headed away, their voices and laughter could be heard for a time, fading to hollow echoes and then silence.

"I notice the schoolmaster hasn't left yet," Brom said angrily.

"I'm sure he'll be out soon," Isabelle said.

"He better be," Brom said.

Finally the door opened and Ichabod Crane exited in a stumbling rush, as if he'd been pushed hard from behind. He turned quickly as if to re-enter, but the door to the house shut hard in his face.

"Katrina!" he called pitifully. "You must know I was jesting."

No sound came from inside. The schoolmaster pushed against the door, but clearly it was fastened. He turned with a sigh and clumped off toward the barn.

Carter turned to look at Brom Bones and

caught another flash of the young man's teeth in the moonlight. His mood had improved when he saw Ichabod so totally dejected.

"I'll be off now, lads," Brom whispered. "I need to get my horse and be on my way. You should head home as well. You never know what haunts and goblins might lurk in the darkness." Brom chuckled and slipped away toward the barn.

Izzy hopped off the rock and grabbed Carter by the wrist. "Looks like it's almost showtime," she said. "We don't want to miss anything."

She dragged Carter toward the barn. A servant leaned on the door frame, his face turned toward the light.

Instead of slipping in through the door, Isabelle pulled Carter over to one of the windows. The shutters were pulled almost closed, but thick bands of light leaked from the bottom and center crack. Carter leaned close and peered into the barn.

Ichabod Crane practically dragged the skinny

horse from the stall, cuffing it twice to try to speed the animal along. Carter gritted his teeth and muttered, "It's not a real horse." Gradually the urge to storm in there and shake the schoolteacher for mistreating the poor, sleepy horse passed.

Ichabod heaved himself awkwardly into the saddle, pushing himself up with so much energy that he nearly pitched over on the other side. Carter heard a bark of laughter from the servant in the doorway, quickly covered with a hoarse cough.

Ichabod glared in the man's direction but didn't bother to speak. He turned the horse's head toward the doorway and clomped out.

"Okay, quick," Izzy whispered. "Time to get a horse."

She dragged Carter around to the front of the barn.

"Evening Master Van Tassel," the servant said, nodding toward Isabelle. "You're not planning to go riding so late are you?"

"A guest has left something behind. I promised Carter Van Ripper a ride home as well," Isabelle said.

The servant nodded. "Do you want me to saddle your horse?" He took a step in the direction of a stall where a lovely reddish horse blinked sleepily at them.

"No, thank you," she said. "I can manage."

"I'll need to put out the lanterns," the servant said as he stifled a yawn. He began lifting lanterns from the rafters and blowing them out. Since there were a lot of lanterns, the light faded slowly as Isabelle hurried to saddle the horse.

Carter was impressed as he watched her dealing with straps and buckles. "I'm glad you're here," he said.

She grinned at him. "Now that's something I'm not sure I've heard you say before." She hopped up into the saddle, then held out her hand. "Time to ride, cousin!"

A DARK RIDE

Carter quickly realized that riding behind Izzy wasn't any more comfortable than riding behind Brom had been. Horses were hard.

"How do we know where Ichabod Crane is?" Carter asked.

"Well, the program knows we're trying to catch up," Izzy said. "Logically, it should let us. We don't want to gallop though, because he could hear us and think we're the Headless Horseman."

"That's okay," Carter said. "I'm not in a big hurry for more galloping."

Their horse quickly climbed the rising road, then it turned to run parallel to a high ridge. Carter could look down on a river far below. He heard a dog bark, muffled and far away.

Finally Isabelle elbowed Carter in the stomach and pointed ahead. He leaned around her and saw the silhouette of the gawky schoolmaster on his bony horse. Ichabod Crane bounced even more in his saddle than Carter.

Ahead of them, a huge tree shadowed the road darkly. "That tree is supposed to be haunted," Izzy whispered.

"By what?" Carter asked.

"I'm not sure I remember," she said. "You'll have to read the story."

Carter gave her a light thump on the shoulder for reminding him that he still had to read when all this was over. The tree looking impossibly old, older than anything Carter had ever seen. The branches were thick as normal tree trunks and they twisted and turned toward the ground as if hoping to snatch riders from their horses.

Carter heard Ichabod begin a nervous whistling. A blast of wind hit the tree just then and the branches creaked and rustled toward the skinny rider. Crane reigned the horse in sharply and stopped whistling. Even from so far away, Carter could see the schoolteacher shaking in the saddle.

Finally Crane seemed to gather up his courage and move along. Izzy continued to follow and now it was their horse within the clutches of the haunted tree. Then they passed under the sweeping branches and Carter held his breath. Surely the story would save the really scary stuff for Ichabod Crane.

Bony fingers raked across Carter's scalp and he yelped, throwing himself away from the tree and clean out of the saddle. He landed on the hard dirt road.

"What are you doing?" Isabelle whispered fiercely.

"Something in the tree tried to grab me," he said.

"It's a tree, Carter," she said, holding out a hand. "It's got branches. One probably just brushed your head because you're so tall."

"Right." Carter didn't believe that for a

second. He got up and brushed the dirt off the seat of his pants. Then he stomped ahead down the road. "I'm not getting back on the horse under that tree."

Isabelle followed him until he felt he'd reached a safe distance from the grabby tree. A small brook crossed the road and Carter didn't want to go wading. He took her offered hand and heaved himself back up onto the horse. Once on again, he learned that falling on your rear does not make horseback riding any more pleasant.

Why are girls so crazy about this? he wondered.

They splashed through the brook and headed into a more heavily wooded patch. Vine-choked trees blocked out the feeble light of the stars and moon, offering only black on black shadows around them. Ichabod Crane was creeping through the woods so slowly that Izzy had to keep their horse tightly reigned to avoid overtaking him.

Then suddenly, the schoolmaster began

kicking his horse in the ribs, shaking the reins and trying to urge it into a run. Instead, old Gunpowder danced sideways and ran his side into a nearby fence, giving Crane's leg a hard enough smack to make him yelp.

Crane shook the reins harder and kicked with the leg not trapped in the fence. The horse merely danced sideways in the other direction, right into a thicket of prickly vines that smacked at the schoolmaster, rumpling his neatly plastered hair into a mess.

Finally, Crane reached behind and smacked Gunpowder in the rear with a thin whip. The horse raced forward toward a small bridge, then slammed to a stop just at the edge of the boards. Crane was thrown forward until he lay nearly full length on the horse's neck.

That's when Carter spotted the huge hulking shadow just to the side of the bridge, coming up from the steep stream banks. In the gloom, he could make out no details, only that the creature was big and coming closer.

Ichabod Crane scooted back down off the horse's neck and into his saddle again. In a voice that squeaked like a rusty hinge, he called, "Who are you?"

The hulking shadow didn't answer.

"Wh-who are you?" he asked again, his voice growing thinner with each attempt to speak.

The hulking shadow still gave no response.

Crane went crazy in a flurry of kicks, smacks, and shaking of reins, but Gunpowder paid him as little mind as the mysterious shadow. The horse stayed as still as a statue.

Ichabod Crane began to sing through his nose. It was a gloomy song with a pace like molasses poured on the ground, but the hulking shadow must have liked it because it climbed the rest of the way onto the road and took a place beside Gunpowder.

Carter could now see the shadowy figure was a man on a horse. The horse was huge and black as the night around it. The man on it wore some kind of heavy cape, but above it, Carter couldn't see the man's head.

"The Headless Horseman," he whispered.

Isabelle nodded but didn't say anything.

The Headless Horseman's approach seemed to finally loosen Gunpowder's legs. The Horseman rode along on the horse's blind side and Gunpowder kept up an easy pace beside him. Crane urged Gunpowder to move faster, but the strange Horseman easily matched his pace. So Crane reined hard, and Gunpowder slowed to a staggering walk. The Horseman slowed with him.

Isabelle's horse clattered over the wooden bridge but neither of the riders ahead seemed to hear it. She carefully kept them at an even distance, though Carter doubted that either the terrified schoolmaster or the Headless Horseman would notice them even if they jumped onto the backs of their two horses.

What played out in front of them was clearly just about Ichabod Crane and the Headless Horseman.

Finally the thick, swampy woods began to thin. Carter could see the Horseman more clearly now. Brom Bones was only a little taller than Carter and the Horseman seemed incredibly tall and broad. Even without a head, he would have been taller than Brom Bones, Carter was sure of it. So if this wasn't a prank played by Brom, was it really a ghost?

Carter saw Crane's storklike nose pointed at the Horseman and the schoolmaster's mouth hung open. In a clear panic, Ichabod Crane began kicking, whipping, and shouting at Gunpowder. The old horse seemed to gather himself up and leap forward, but the Horseman had no trouble leaping right at the skinny horse's side.

The horses were in full gallop now and Isabelle dug her feet into her own horse's side to give chase. Carter had to hang on tightly to avoid being bounced off the horse's rear. He peeked over his cousin's shoulder as she leaned over the horse's neck.

Carter realized he could almost recognize the road ahead. He was pretty sure it was the one that led to the schoolhouse eventually. The schoolmaster's oversized clothes flapped around him as the horse galloped. Both horses kicked up stones and sparks as they ran.

Like Izzy, Crane leaned forward, practically laying on the horse's neck to urge its speed. But unlike Izzy, his rear bounced in the saddle.

Carter was impressed by the speed the scrawny horse managed against the black monster riding along beside it. Then he saw the road divide up ahead with a slow easy climb upward and a sharp turn to the left. Clearly the Horseman expected Ichabod Crane to stay on the road to the schoolhouse. Instead, Gunpowder turned sharply and plunged downhill.

Isabelle made the turn easily and now their

horse was actually between Ichabod Crane and the Headless Horseman! Carter heard the black horse pounding behind them while Gunpowder kept his wild lead.

Then Carter saw Crane's saddle slipping under him. The schoolmaster made a grab for it but he couldn't hold it in place, not while he sat on it! Finally, he threw himself forward, wrapping his arms around Gunpowder's long neck. This put Crane's rear quarters high in the air and the saddle simply slipped out from under him and landed in the road just ahead of Carter and Izzy.

Their horse spooked at the sudden appearance of the flopping, bouncing saddle. The horse reared and Izzy hung on, but Carter tumbled off the backside of their horse with the same grace as the schoolmaster's saddle. He landed hard on the road and then rolled to the right and threw his arms over his head.

He heard the Horseman's monster horse

rear and snort above him. With his eyes tightly closed, Carter wondered what a simulated horse trampling would feel like. He bet it was going to hurt.

THE WILD RIDE ENDS

Carter felt the ground shake close to him as the black horse dropped back to four legs and raced off. He sat up and looked around just as more hoofbeats sounded around him.

"Come on!" Isabelle yelled.

Carter made out her pale face against the night. He reached up and grabbed her hand as she pulled her foot out of the nearest stirrup so he could use it to get himself back up on the horse. As soon as he settled again, Izzy kicked the horse's ribs and they joined the chase.

Without a saddle, Ichabod's riding had turned into a comedy. Sometimes he shifted so far to the side that Carter was sure he would fall. Then the schoolmaster would hoist himself back up using Gunpowder's mane, only to slide in the other direction.

"We're coming up on the church," Isabelle yelled.

Carter peered past her and saw that the tree line was thinning. He thought he could see the white of a building between the trees ahead. He remembered Brom's story of how the Horseman stopped at a bridge near the church. Carter saw how the brook was beginning to crowd the side of the road. Were they almost to the point where the brook crossed the road? Was the ride almost over?

Ichabod Crane seemed to think so. Carter noticed the schoolmaster sat up a bit straighter, as if finally feeling a surge of confidence. But the Horseman was closing in fast, as Gunpowder began to slow slightly. Crane must have felt the Horseman's closeness or heard the thundering hooves, because he gave Gunpowder a hard kick in the ribs.

The old horse leaped onto an old wooden bridge and Carter could hear the bang of the hooves against the planks. The Horseman followed Crane onto the bridge, but Crane made it to the other side first. He turned his horse to look back at the Horseman, clearly expecting him to vanish in a clap of lightning as the stories promised.

Instead, the Horseman stopped in the middle of the bridge. The rider reigned in the huge beast so hard that the horse reared and pawed at the sky. Then Carter saw the Horseman scoop something out of his lap. It looked exactly the right size for a head. The Horseman raised up in his stirrups and hurled the head at Ichabod Crane!

In the moonlight, Carter could see the schoolmaster's eyes grow round as the head flew at him. At the last second, Crane turned and urged Gunpowder forward, but it was too late. The Horseman's head struck Ichabod Crane in the back of his own flat-topped skull, just below his hat.

The impact drove Ichabod Crane headlong

over Gunpowder's neck. He landed hard in the dust. The old horse gathered himself and jumped over the schoolmaster. The Horseman's steed leaped over the body as well, then turned and stopped for the Horseman to look at what he had done.

Isabelle had reined in as well. Carter and Izzy waited silently on the opposite side of the bridge. They watched as the black horse danced around in the dust. Then, the Horseman sat up and turned toward them. Neither the Horseman nor Carter or Izzy moved for a moment.

Finally, the Horseman gathered his reins and ran at them. Izzy shrieked and wrestled the reins, which apparently was a little too much for the horse. It reared up in a panic and Carter hit the ground again, but this time Izzy landed on him.

The horse raced away and the Horseman laughed. The sound seemed to echo around them, deep and almost crazy. Then the

Horseman raced by and disappeared into the night.

"Are you okay?" Izzy asked.

"I'll be better when you get off me," Carter answered. She scrambled to his side, stood up, and dusted off her clothes while she looked down at him.

"I want to go check on Crane." She held out her hand.

Carter moaned as she helped him up. "This adventure has been hard on my rump. How did you survive horseback riding lessons?"

"You get used to it," she said. She was already turned toward the bridge. Carter figured he didn't have a choice, he had to go look for more trouble with her.

As they tromped across the bridge, the wind howled through the hollow, sounding like a pack of wolves. "Are you sure there are no werewolves in this story?" he asked.

"I'm sure there are no werewolves in any of the books on Uncle Dan's computer," she said.

"Well, that stinks," he grumbled. Not that he wanted to run into werewolves tonight. But he'd like to run into werewolves sometime. "Are there any more ghosts or vampires or monsters—you know, cool stuff?"

"Yes, yes, and yes," she said as they crossed the bridge. "Plus lots of cool stuff. Just no werewolves. Though I read an essay once that said Doctor Jekyll and Mr. Hyde was really the first werewolf novel, but I think that's pushing it. And there's the *Hound of the Baskervilles*, of course. The hound was huge and had glowing jowls and eyes."

"Have you read all the books?" he asked.

She shook her head. "Mostly, but I never read *Treasure Island*. It's on Uncle Dan's computer, but I don't like pirates."

"I thought every girl liked Johnny Depp," Carter said.

"He's an actor," she said in that smartie pants voice that Carter hated most. "He's not really a pirate."

They had reached the far side of the bridge. They fell silent a moment while they scanned the ground for Ichabod Crane. They saw some shadowy pieces of something, but the schoolmaster was gone.

"Wow, where do you think he went?" Carter asked. "He hit the ground pretty hard."

"I don't know." She looked around and pointed. "Maybe the graveyard or the church."

"Yeah, if I were a great big chicken, I would run for the graveyard in the dark right after some ghost threw its head at me."

"It wasn't a head," she said, pointing at the ground as they got close. In the light from the moon, he saw big broken shards of pumpkin and a half-squashed hat. It was the hat Ichabod Crane had been wearing during the crazy ride.

"So should we look around the church for Crane?" Carter asked.

"I don't think we'd find him," his cousin said. "According to the book, no one ever saw Ichabod Crane in this area again. Brom's prank scared him away for good."

"So it was Brom, for sure? I know he talked about playing a prank on Crane but that was pretty extreme. And that laugh didn't sound like Brom. It was crazy."

Isabelle shrugged. "The story doesn't say for sure."

"Is the story over?"

Isabelle shrugged again. "Basically."

"Then why are we standing here in the dark with crickets chirping and a breeze blowing off the brook? Why aren't we standing in really dark virtual reality suits as they split open at the back and let us out to get some lunch?" Carter's voice climbed a bit at the end since he was getting really hungry.

"I'm not sure." Izzy walked across the churchyard and sat down on the low piled stone wall that circled the graveyard. Carter followed her but didn't sit down. First, he wasn't sure his rear would really enjoy sitting. And second, he really didn't want to sit with his back to a creepy cemetery.

"Could you have missed some kind of hack from Storm?" Carter asked. He felt shaky even thinking about that. Storm's hacks on *Alice in Wonderland* had involved a lot of sharp objects and a lot of running on his part.

"No, I'm absolutely sure I didn't miss anything," Isabelle said firmly. "Okay, we don't see Ichabod Crane anymore but the story does tell us that boys showed up at the school in the morning and ran wild since the schoolmaster never showed up. That was the first clue that he was missing."

"So we're stuck here until morning?" Carter wrapped his arms around his stomach and wondered how long it took to starve to death. "If we are, I am not going back to the Van Ripper house. You got the nice dad in this story. I'm betting that Van Ripper guy doesn't mind smacking people once in a while."

"It could be worse than that," Isabelle whispered. "The story also tells us about Brom's wedding to Katrina."

"We're stuck here until they get married!" Carter's voice sounded a little shrieky even to his ears.

"Worse," Isabelle said. "A farmer discovered Ichabod Crane living somewhere else years later."

"Years! We can't last years in here!" Now Carter was just yelling. "We have to get out of here. Maybe . . . maybe if we really moved around a lot, it would pop the back of the suit open."

Carter began flailing his arms and stretching his long legs up as high as he could. He swung his arms forward, trying to stretch his back as much as possible. He tried stretching every way he possibly could, even flinging himself on the ground in an effort to stretch in more ways.

"Why aren't you trying this?" Carter asked, glaring at Isabelle.

"First, you look whacked," she said. "Second, if it works for you, you can just turn the program off and let me out. So I don't have to roll around on the ground like that. Third, if anyone saw you, they'd think you were possessed and our life here would get even weirder."

Carter flopped over in exhaustion. "It's not working anyway."

"You know, Uncle Dan is a pretty careful programmer," Isabelle said. "He must have a way out of the program. It just doesn't make sense that he didn't build in an exit."

"Well, where is it?" Carter asked.

"I don't know," she snapped back. "You're the one who is better at connecting with Uncle Dan's mysterious side. If you were going to hide an exit, what would you do? We haven't exactly run across any big doors with glowing exit signs over them."

Carter didn't answer for a moment. Something about what she'd just said struck a memory. Why was that? Then it hit him and he grinned.

"Actually, maybe we did."

THROUGH THE WOODS

"**W**hat are you talking about?" Isabelle asked.

"It's in the schoolhouse. Think about it," Carter said. "There was a skinny door up near the end of the building. I noticed it when I first came in. It had an x scratched in it."

Isabelle frowned, clearly trying to remember. "How do you know it wasn't a closet?"

"First, it had an x. That's for exit."

"Exit doesn't start with an x."

"I know that." He huffed in annoyance at his cousin. "But it sounds like it does. And besides, think about it. I came into the building through a door in that same wall. It's just a big log box. How could that door go to a closet? I know it doesn't go outside, I would have seen the door on the outside wall." He grinned. "It's an impossible door."

Isabelle nodded and hopped off the wall. "Now that's logic I can agree with."

"So how do we get to the school from here?" Carter asked as he gestured into the darkness. "Back down the road?"

"We could get there that way, but I think there's a shorter route," Isabelle said slowly. "I don't think you're going to like it."

"I love the idea of a shorter way," Carter said. "I'm tired and hungry and I'm pretty sure I fell off a horse a million times today."

"It's through the cemetery."

"I hate that idea," he said. "We're in the middle of a ghost story that features spooks in that very cemetery. And you want to walk through it in the dark? This is not a good idea."

"It's shorter," she said. "If we go by the road, the program has to maintain the logic of what we've seen. So it'll be just as long as it was when we rode on it. If we go through the cemetery, the program could let us reach the school way faster."

Carter moaned. "Okay, we go through the cemetery. I'll just keep thinking about raiding Uncle Dan's fridge when we finally get out of here. That should keep my stomach growling loud enough to scare away any ghost."

As they climbed over the low wall, the moon slipped behind a cloud and the night grew much darker. Then when they took their first step into the cemetery, a gust of wind blew through the gravestones with a low moan.

"I hate this idea," Carter muttered again.

"Think about the fridge," Isabelle said as she began threading her way through the thin headstones.

The stones were thin and rough. In the darkness, there was no way to read any of the names carved into them. Some of the stones were unusually short and Carter tripped over one, stumbling several steps and smacking his knee on another headstone before finally getting his balance.

"Why did they sneak in these short stones? They're dangerous."

"They probably mark the graves of little kids," Isabelle said. "It was pretty hard to survive childhood a long time ago."

"Oh." Carter felt kind of bad for grumbling about the poor kids' markers. Another moaning wind slipped between the stones, and Carter felt the small hairs stand up on his neck.

"You don't think there's a ghost out here do you?" he asked.

"They certainly talked about ghosts at the party," Isabelle said. "Wasn't one of them known for moaning?"

"And shrieking," Carter said. "The woman in white."

A shriek burst from the dark night and Isabelle answered it with one of her own. "You had to mention shrieking," she said as she looked around for the source of the sound. Isabelle continued forward. "That didn't sound like the wind. Do you think it could be a puma? I think I read they shriek."

"A puma? And you're mad at me for giving the program ideas? At least the woman in white didn't eat anyone!" Carter replied.

The night must have been growing cloudy because now it was hard even to see stars. The graveyard was only a blur of low, black shapes against the faintly lighter black night. Carter was finding it harder and harder to find his footing. Plus huge trees seemed to hunch over them in places, which meant thin branches raked his head repeatedly.

"I'd give a lot for a flashlight right about now," Carter mumbled.

Isabelle stopped walking so quickly that Carter plowed into the back of her. "Hey, that's a good idea. I wonder if we can give the program that idea." She paused a moment, then said very clearly. "Don't I hear a creaking noise? I think the caretaker has left his lantern hanging from one of these trees."

To Carter's surprise, he did hear a creak. He crept forward and the sound grew louder. When it seemed right in front of him, he reached out and found the lantern hanging from the tree.

"That's just too cool," he said. "Now if we just had a match."

"It's a good thing you have that flint and striker in your pocket," she said loudly.

He stuck his hand in the deep pocket of his jacket and found a piece of rock and a piece of oddly twisted metal. "Do you know how to use one of these?"

"You knock the metal against the rock and it throws a spark. You do it next to the wick and it should light the lantern," she said. "Don't you remember the Colonial Days field trip back in fourth grade?"

"I remember that I had to sit next to Austin," Carter said. "And I think his mom only feeds him beans. I clearly remember the smell. Everything after that is pretty hazy." He handed the lantern to Isabelle. "Here, you hold this part, and I'll try to strike a spark."

"Let me raise the chimney first and turn up some wick," she said, fumbling with the lantern. "Okay, you'll need to put the spark close to the wick so feel for it first."

Carter reached out and accidentally bopped Isabelle on the nose, making her drop the lantern. "Sorry," he said, bending down to grab it and knocking heads with her. "Ouch, I can't see anything."

"I've got it," she said, sounding a little stuffy. "I'm holding the lantern in front of my face now. I should be safer with it between you and me. Just feel for the wick, gently."

He reached out more slowly this time and found the small bit of cotton string. Then he held the rock close to the string and smacked it with the twisted metal. A spark flashed. It took two more tries before the wick lit and they finally had light.

The light of the lantern created a pool around them, pushing back the darkness. "That's a lot better," Carter said, just as another moan swept the cemetery. "Now let's get out of here. I'm really done with ghost stories for today."

They slipped through the gravestones more quickly with the light. Carter only smacked his leg a half dozen times before he spotted the outer wall of the cemetery.

"Finally," he said, picking up his pace. "It should be clear sailing now."

That was when a shriek rang out again behind them. They both whirled to see a glowing figure drifting toward them through the graves. It was a woman in a long, white gown that hung in tatters on her nearly skeletal body. Her pale hair hung to her waist in clumps. Her face was long, but that might have been because her mouth was stretched into an impossibly long oval.

The figure ended at the ragged hem of her dress and floated slightly above the ground as she moved toward them. Although she glowed and the lantern light fell on her, Carter couldn't see her eyes at all. They were just two black holes in her face. As she moved, her fingers flexed. Her nails were long and curved like claws. And she screamed again.

It was the last scream that unfroze Carter and Isabelle. They ran the few yards to the wall and leaped up and over as if they had springs on their feet. They continued to run hard, slapping at low-hanging branches and jumping over the scattered rocks that tried to trip them.

Finally they burst from the tree line and faced the short road to the schoolhouse. They slowed to a walk, both watching the trees sharply for any more surprises. The night sounds now were much more normal, just crickets and the low hoot of an owl.

"I hope you're right about the exit," Isabelle said, panting. "Because I'm really tired of this book."

Carter laughed. "Now that's something I've never heard you say before."

X MARKS THE EXIT

They walked as quickly as exhaustion would let them.

Carter held up the lantern to light the road, but they still stumbled several times.

"Next time we do this," Carter said, "let's check the exits first."

"Right," Isabelle mumbled beside him.

He looked down at her as she shuffled up the hill. "Are you okay?"

"Tired," she said. "Hungry. I'll be fine if the exit really is in the schoolhouse."

Carter agreed. He picked up his pace a little, eager to get to Uncle Dan's fridge. When he reached the door, he pulled hard but nothing happened. He shook and rattled it. Then he kicked it until his toes hurt.

Isabelle leaned on the schoolhouse wall. "Right, Ichabod Crane started locking up the schoolhouse after Brom and his friends wrecked it one night."

"That's super," Carter said, giving the door one more hard kick. Then he perked up. "Some of the windows are just covered with paper. I can climb through."

Isabelle shook her head. "They have some kind of inner shutters fastened with loops of vine and stakes, I think."

"I'm going to check anyway. He was in a big hurry to get to the party. He might have forgotten." Carter walked around the school, trying each window. He punched through the paper coverings, but each time, he ran into a closed shutter. He pounded on the shutters until his hands hurt as much as his toes, but none swung in.

Finally he had circled the whole building and found Isabelle still leaning on the wall. He peered closer at the door. It had a rough iron fastening and keyhole, which seemed pretty fancy for a building that looked like an oversized shed.

"We could try to pick the lock," he suggested.

Isabelle perked up slightly. "With what?"

Carter fished the metal loop out of his pocket. The ends tapered a bit though they were far from pointed, but the keyhole was huge compared to his front door at home. "Here, hold the lantern."

Isabelle held it while Carter shoved the thinner end of the metal into the hole. He wiggled and waggled for a bit until he felt something move slightly inside. He slid the bit of metal gently, trying to lever the inner workings. But the part of the iron striker that was thin enough to fit in the keyhole was just too short. He could nudge the workings a little but he couldn't quite get them to move.

He kept trying until he felt like screaming in frustration. Finally he jerked the iron striker out of his pocket and threw it into the night. "It doesn't work!" he howled. "We need a key."

Isabelle stared in the direction he'd thrown

the bit of metal. "I hope we don't need a fire before we figure a way out of here," she said. She sighed deeply and slid until she was sitting on the rocky ground next to the wall. "I guess we're stuck until morning when the students come."

"Does the story say any of the students got into the schoolhouse?" Carter asked.

"Let me think." She closed her eyes and leaned against the wall. Finally she opened them. "I don't remember."

"But maybe one of them could have a key. After all, one of the fathers might want the boy to have a key in case Ichabod Crane is late. Especially in bad weather." Carter paced a little as he talked. "It would probably be the oldest son of the wealthiest farmer. Let's see, Van Tassel has pull around here. So maybe your dad gave you a key just in case Ichabod Crane came in late after an evening of courting your sister. Maybe it's even in your pocket right now. A nice, big, iron key."

Isabelle stood up, joining in the idea eagerly. "Of course Father would give me such a key." She held her hand over the jacket pocket for a second, as if scared to reach for it. Then, she plunged her hand into the pocket and pulled out the key.

Carter whooped with joy and they danced around in the moonlight in a sudden burst of energy. Then Isabelle shoved the key in the lock and turned. The door swung open on the deep darkness of the classroom.

"There aren't any stories about ghosts in the classroom are there?" Carter asked as he held up the lantern and stared into the shadows.

"Nope, Ichabod Crane was the only horror in here," she said.

Carter swung the lantern around and they both spotted the narrow door near the schoolmaster's desk. As Carter remembered, a deep x was carved into the wood, but now a faint light glowed through the gouges.

"Okay, that's a little creepy," he said.

"If it'll get us out of this program, it's beautiful to me," Isabelle said as she wrenched open the door. The space beyond was lit by a nearly blinding white light. No details of floor or walls were visible with so much light. Isabelle giggled.

"Walk toward the light, Carter. Walk toward the light," she said in her best spooky ghost story voice.

He gave her a light shove. "Ladies first."

They stepped out of the classroom and into the blinding light. Then the lights went out, plunging them into a dark more profound than anything they'd experience in Sleepy Hollow.

Carter yelped and tried to step back. That's when he was aware of the suit around him. He could feel the gloves against his fingers and his knees against the joints of the space suit pants. He pressed his back against the suit seam and it opened, leaking light into the suit.

Carter scrambled out so fast he lost his balance and once more slammed his rear into the floor. "Ow," he howled. "I'm not going to be able to sit comfortably for a week."

Isabelle leaned over him and offered him a hand up. "This is getting to be a habit."

"Yeah, one I'm definitely breaking," he said. "Thanks."

"Last one to the fridge has to eat veggies," Isabelle said as she spun and sprinted for the door.

Carter dashed after her, they were neck and neck on the stairs, where it's hard to pass. But then, Isabelle spotted a pile of mail under the front door's mail slot. She slowed to scoop it up and Carter passed her. It was smooth sailing from there.

Uncle Dan's freezer was always full of microwave pizza and corn dogs. Carter held out the "veggie supreme" box to Isabelle. "And you have to eat the veggies," he said.

"It works for me, as long as it's pizza." She tore open the box and slid the pizza onto a plate with a clink. "You know you only won because

I got Uncle Dan's mail."

"The important thing is I won." Carter grinned as he closed the door on the microwave and set the time. Then he snagged a soda from the fridge and popped the top, guzzling half the can and executing the world's most perfect barking burp.

"You're disgusting," Isabelle said as she flipped through the mail. "Hey, we got a card from Uncle Dan." She held it up.

Carter hurried over to the look at the postcard. The picture showed a storm at sea, buffeting a lighthouse. Isabelle flipped it over and Carter checked the date first: 12/25/1999. That date didn't mean Uncle Dan was really slow in mailing out his Christmas cards. It was the clue for picking the code words out of the message. Each digit pointed at the location of the code word in the sentence.

Isabelle laid the card on the counter and as they read their uncle's cramped printing, Carter underlined each code word:

Storm blew us off course for a while. I *located* the small island where the best fishing can be found. A *confrontation* between the captain and I made things tense for a while. But it is fine *and* we're friends again. *Capture* some crickets for me. I am certain that another fishing trip is *imminent*. Though it will certainly be good to be *home*. I am sure I will talk to you *soon*.

"He's found the hacker," Isabelle said.

Carter nodded and grinned. "Go, Uncle Dan!"

Isabelle nodded as Carter turned back to the microwave to hurry his pizza along, but her eyebrows still furrowed with worry. "Be careful, Uncle Dan," she whispered.

"What?" Carter asked.

"I said, 'Eat while you can,'" Isabelle said. "After this, you have to go home and read the book."

Carter took another swallow of soda and burped at her. "Actually, laying on my nice, soft bed with a book sounds pretty good."

Isabelle opened her mouth to respond to that and Carter pointed at her. "Don't bother saying it. You're right. That isn't something you hear from me very often."

Isabelle grinned, laying Uncle Dan's postcard back on the counter as the microwave dinged. "You never know what you'll hear around this place. Now make way for the veggie pizza. I'm starved."

The suits are working properly now, and Uncle Dan thinks he's found Storm. But this is just the calm before the storm for Carter, Isabelle, and Uncle Dan!

Follow the adventure in

Book 3
Trapped in Stormy Seas
Sailing to Treasure Island